The *Supernatural* Quiz Book Season 5

500 questions and answers on *Supernatural* Season 5

Light Bulb Quizzes

Written by fans, for fans

Unofficial

Published by Light Bulb Quizzes

ISBN 978-0-9932030-4-6

Edited by
Kim Kimber
www.kimkimber.co.uk

Cover artwork by
White Tree Fine Art
www.facebook.com/whitetreefineart
www.whitetreefineart.co.uk

All of the questions in this quiz book are based on the DVD release of *Supernatural* Season 5, produced by Warner Home Video and the soundtrack and other details may sometimes vary from that of other versions.

This book is unofficial and unauthorised. All of the questions have been researched and compiled by Light Bulb Quizzes who have done their best to ensure that all information is correct. However, if any sharp-eyed *Supernatural* fans notice an error, please contact us so that it can be rectified.

For all fans of
Supernatural

CONTENTS

Introduction

Light Bulb Quizzes is pleased to continue its look back at the *Supernatural* series with a further 500 questions and answers, this time all about Season 5.

In *Supernatural* Season 5, Dean (Jensen Ackles), Sam (Jared Padalecki) and Castiel (Misha Collins) join forces as Team Free Will and go up against the Four Horsemen of the Apocalypse. Lucifer (Mark Pellegrino), freed from his cage, wreaks chaos upon the earth and begins his torment of Sam, we meet the 'King of Hell', Crowley (Mark Sheppard), for the first time and Death (Julian Richings) makes his unforgettable, dramatic entrance. Season 5 also sees Ellen and Jo bravely sacrifice their lives to save the Winchester brothers (Dean and Sam).

A strong storyline, well-written scripts, quality actors and the chemistry between the main characters make this another unforgettable season. Light Bulb Quizzes happily admits that Season 5 is one of our personal favourites and we have spent far too much time re-watching past episodes.

As always the questions in this book have been researched and compiled by fans for the *Supernatural* family to enjoy. As with our previous quiz books, *The Supernatural Quiz Book Season 5* aims to give fans an opportunity to revisit their favourite moments and find out more about all those memorable characters from seasons past and the actors who so skilfully brought them to life.

We hope, like us, that you will enjoy taking another nostalgic look back at the *road so far…*

Light Bulb Quizzes

Written by fans, for fans

'Team Free Will. One ex-blood junkie,
one dropout with 6 bucks to his name, and
Mr. Comatose over there. Awesome.' ~
Dean Winchester

Questions

Episode 1 – Sympathy for the Devil

1. Where does the episode begin?

2. What happens to the doors when Dean and Sam run for them?

3. Where do Dean and Sam end up after the blistering white light appears?

4. What happens next?

5. What does Chuck say happened to Castiel?

6. Why do the Archangels say they need to kill Lucifer quickly?

7. What does Sam make and give to Dean?

8. Who is writing fan fiction and then gets a call from Chuck?

9. Who 'booted Lucifer's ass to the basement' (put Lucifer in his cage)?

10. How does Dean discover where Michael's sword is hidden?

11. Why doesn't demon Bobby kill Dean?

12. Who has been chosen to be Michael's vessel – Dean, Sam or Bobby?

13. Zachariah tortures Dean and Sam with different illnesses, who saves them?

14. Who is Nick?

15. What do the doctors tell Bobby?

Episode 2 – Good God, Y'All

16. Why can't Castiel heal Bobby?

17. Castiel tells Dean and Sam that he plans to do what?

18. What does Castiel want to borrow from Dean and Sam?

19. Who rings Bobby and why?

20. Who turns up and points a gun at the Winchester brothers?

21. Who is the above hunting with when Rufus calls?

22. Why does Dean ask Sam to hold back?

23. What is different when Sam stabs the demons?

24. Who attacks Sam and Ellen at the 'demon basecamp'?

25. What do Jo and Rufus think Sam is?

26. The events in the town are a sign of what?

27. How does War control events and create hallucinations?

28. What car does War drive?

29. How do Dean and Sam stop War?

30. What does Sam feel he now needs to do?

Episode titles

Can you name the Season 5 episode titles from the clues?

31. Part of the inscription over the gates of hell in Dante's *Inferno.*

32. A reference to a best-selling memoir by Susanna Kaysen, later made into a movie in which Misha Collins had a role.

33. Title of a song by English heavy metal band, Iron Maiden.

34. Lyric from a Whitney Houston song.

35. Famous song by The Doors used in the soundtrack of the iconic 1979 movie *Apocalypse Now.*

36. Title of the 1973 studio album by English rock band, Pink Floyd.

37. Jensen Ackles starred in a 2009 3D remake of a film with this title.

38. A final performance before retirement or death, also the title of an episode of *Gilmore Girls*, starring Jared Padalecki.

39. Biography of English rock band, Led Zeppelin, by American music journalist, Stephen Davis.

40. Adapted from the title of a story by F. Scott Fitzgerald, later a movie starring Brad Pitt.

41. A song by British rock band, The Rolling Stones, later covered by American band Guns N' Roses.

42. Single by Jay Z, released in 2004, title denotes the 99th episode of *Supernatural.*

43.   Derived from a well-known 'devil' saying.

44.   Led Zeppelin song and also the title of an episode of *Dawson's Creek* featuring Jensen Ackles.

45.   A 1982 film noir parody starring Steve Martin.

Episode 3 – Free to Be You and Me

46. Who appears to Sam at night?

47. What does Sam burn in the sink?

48. Whilst Dean is away hunting what does Sam start working as?

49. Who creeps up on Dean in the bathroom?

50. Who does Castiel need help finding?

51. What does Dean give Castiel?

52. Where does Dean take Castiel?

53. Who visits Sam at the bar?

54. True or false: Dean and Castiel use a ring of burning holy oil to trap Raphael?

55. Sam tells Lindsey that he used to be in business with whom?

56. What does Raphael say about God?

57. Who is 'Jessica' in reality?

58. Who does Lucifer say is his one true vessel – Dean, Sam or Castiel?

59. What do the demons try to force-feed Sam at the bar?

60. Dean refers to Raphael as what kind of fictional teenage character?

Episode 4 – The End

61. Who is Dean talking to on the phone at the beginning of the episode?

62. What does Dean find funny?

63. Who rings whilst Dean is sleeping and what is his news?

64. Where does Dean wake up and what year has he woken up in?

65. Who appears in the car next to Dean, reading a newspaper – Castiel, Zachariah or Sam?

66. What does Dean discover at Bobby's house?

67. When Dean arrives at the camp, who knocks him unconscious?

68. What does 2009 Dean tell future Dean that only they would know?

69. Who wants to talk to Dean?

70. What is Castiel doing when Dean finds him?

71. Why does future Dean shoot a man who has been on the mission with him?

72. Why is future Dean taking 2009 Dean on the mission to kill the devil?

73. What colour suit is Lucifer wearing?

74. Who rescues 2009 Dean from Zachariah?

75. True or false: Dean and Sam make amends at the end of the episode and agree to hunt together again?

Supernatural Quotes

Who said the following during Supernatural Season 5:

76. 'This is one little planet in one tiny solar system in a galaxy that's barely out of its diapers. I'm old, Dean. Very old. So I invite you to contemplate how insignificant I find you.'

77. 'They keep this guy chained in a box six hundred feet under. Last time they hauled him up, Noah was building a boat. That's why the place is crawling with reapers. They're waiting on the big boss to show.'

78. 'Some free advice? You ever get back there, you hoard toilet paper. You understand me? Hoard it. Hoard it like it's made of gold. 'cause it is.'

79. 'So, the Hardy boys finally tracked me down. Took you long enough.'

80. 'Yeah well, I guess the monster that ate me didn't get that memo.'

81. 'Yeah, life as an angel condom. That's real fun.'

82. 'You know, my brother... I practically raised him. I took care of him in a way most people could never understand, and I still love him. But I am going to kill him, because it is right, and I have to.'

83. 'Our lives suck. But Sam and Dean. To wake up every morning and save the world. To have a brother who would die for you. Well, who wouldn't want that?'

84.   'I'm waiting to hook up with my siblings. I've got three. We're going to have so much fun together.'

85.   'It's not them. It's me. It's inside me. I'm mad... all the time... and I don't know why.'

86.   'He's my husband. My job is to bring him peace… not pain.'

87.   'Jared and Jensen are two of the nicest guys you could meet…'

88.   'Look Sam. I'm not gonna lie. We had undeniable chemistry. But like a monkey on the sun it was too hot to live. It can't go on.'

89.   'God did this to you, Nick. And I can give you justice. Peace.'

90.   'It actually means, "you, um, breed with the mouth of a goat." It's funnier in Enochian.'

Episode 5 – Fallen Idols

91. Whose car does the man in the opening sequence claim to have found?

92. What is the name of the car?

93. What happens when he sits in the car?

94. What agents do Dean and Sam pose as, named after famous drummers?

95. Why does Dean go underneath the 'cursed' car?

96. True or false: The car is genuine and did indeed belong to its famous owner?

97. Who kills the next victim?

98. Where do Dean and Sam visit to research the case?

99. What do all the exhibits have that is unusual?

100. Whose ghost attacks Sam?

101. What famous socialite and actress do the girls say took their friend?

102. What does Sam find in the victims' stomachs?

103. What is the name of the pagan god responsible for all the deaths?

104. Who does the above, disguised as Paris Hilton, say is Dean's idol?

105. What film, featuring Jared Padalecki and Paris Hilton, is referenced in this episode?

Episode 6 – I Believe the Children Are Our Future

106. What does the babysitter find in the wardrobe?

107. What do the boy's parents discover?

108. According to the post mortem how did the above die?

109. What prank does the boy admit to?

110. What causes the death of the next victim?

111. What does Dean do with the above 'weapon'?

112. Why does the little girl not want to put her tooth under her pillow?

113. What did she do after her dad had gone to bed?

114. What happens to her dad?

115. What does Dean discover at the hospital?

116. Having pinpointed the farm at the centre of the strange events, who do Dean and Sam find there?

117. True or false: The above was adopted at birth?

118. When they find the mother of the above what does she tell the boys?

119. What does Castiel want to do to Jesse?

120. What happens to Jesse at the end of episode?

Cast Appearances

121. Which of the Four Horsemen of the Apocalypse does actor Matt Frewer play in *Supernatural* Season 5 – War, Famine, Pestilence or Death?

122. What role does actor Matthew Cohen play in episode 13 'The Song Remains the Same'?

123. Actor Hal Ozsan who plays a 900-year-old witch in episode 7 'The Curious Case of Dean Winchester' also took on the role of Miles Cannon in which TV drama in 2010?

124. Can you name the actress who plays Becky Rosen and first appears in Season 5 episode 1 'Sympathy for the Devil?

125. Can you name the angel played by actor Roger Aaron Brown in episode 16 'Dark Side of the Moon'?

126. What controversial American model, singer and actress appeared in episode 5 'Fallen Idols'?

127. Actor John Gries plays the role of retired hunter Martin Creaser in episode 11 'Sam Interrupted' but in what American TV drama did he appear as Roger Linus?

128. Actor Lex Medlin plays which famous cherub in *Supernatural* Season 5?

129. What role do actors Sean Campbell, Colin Lawrence and Scott Michael Campbell play in episode 3 'Free to Be Me and You'?

130. In episode 17 '99 Problems' actress Kayla Mae Maloney plays the role of Leah Gideon, also known as what creature from hell?

131. Actors Devin Ratray and Ernie Grunwald play what roles in episode 9 'The Real Ghostbusters'?

132. In what American TV law drama did actor Titus Welliver, who plays War in *Supernatural* Season 5, appear as Glen Childs during 2009-11?

133. True or false: Carrie Ann Fleming plays the role of Bobby Singer's daughter in episode 15 'Dead Men Don't Wear Plaid'?

134. What role do actors Colton James, Sarah Drew and Alex Arsenault play in episode 12 'Swap Meat'?

135. What actor plays the role of Famine in *Supernatural* Season 5?

Episode 7 – The Curious Case of Dean Winchester

136. What curious event is happening to people in the beginning of this episode?

137. How does Sam identify the missing man, Cliff Whitlow?

138. What nationality is Patrick?

139. How many years does Bobby lose in the poker game – 5, 15 or 25?

140. True or false: Patrick tells Dean that he can buy back Bobby's years?

141. Who is the old man that Sam finds in his hotel room?

142. Why can't Dean crack the code and open the safe?

143. What does Patrick give Sam when he claps his hands three times?

144. Who gives Dean a reversal spell?

145. Does Patrick allow the elderly man, Ash, to have extra years?

146. What does Bobby tell old Dean that he is suffering from when he complains that his back hurts whilst digging?

147. Why doesn't the reversal spell work?

148. Who wins the poker game between Patrick and Sam?

149. Why does Lia help Dean and Sam?

150. How does Lia die?

Episode 8 – Changing Channels

151. What are the Winchester brothers riding in the opening scene?

152. What is Mrs Randolf's Christian name – Katie, Cathy or Karen?

153. What TV character does she think she has seen?

154. What does Sam find at the crime scene?

155. Who do Dean and Sam believe is responsible for the murder of Bill Randolf?

156. What is the name of the TV show that the brothers find themselves in, which Dean is a fan of?

157. How long does the Trickster say Dean and Sam must survive before they can talk to him?

158. Can you name the game in Changing Channels that the brothers are in?

159. Who appears to help Dean and Sam but is banished by the Trickster?

160. True or false: Dean and Sam are staying at the Bay 2 Hotel?

161. Which side does the Trickster say that he is on, heaven or hell?

162. What is Sam turned into?

163. How do Dean and Sam trap the Trickster?

164. Which Archangel are they dealing with?

165. Which one of the Winchester brothers does Gabriel compare to Lucifer?

Rob Benedict (Chuck Shurley)

166. What is Rob's middle name?

167. In what year was Rob born?

168. Rob was born in which country – Canada, USA or Australia?

169. Can you name Rob's actress sister?

170. Rob received a BA degree from Northwestern University, in what subject?

171. Early in his career, Rob developed a one man stage show, based on the life of which iconic movie actor?

172. In which American TV comedy series did Rob play the role of Jeremy Berger in 2008-9?

173. What is the name of the indie rock band that Rob is the lead singer of?

174. Can you name the studio album that Rob released with the above band in 2009?

175. True or false: Rob appeared in two episodes of *Buffy the Vampire Slayer* in 2000?

176. In 2009, Rob played the role of Milt in which movie starring Russell Crowe, Ben Affleck and Helen Mirren?

177. Can you name the character Rob played in the TV series *Felicity*?

178. How many children does Rob have with his wife, Mollie?

179. Rob plays an active role in *Supernatural*
conventions, often appearing with which other
Supernatural actor?

180. Rob's character, Chuck Shurley, writes under which
pen name in *Supernatural*?

Episode 9 – The Real Ghostbusters

181. What is the name of the hotel in the opening sequence – The Pinewood Hotel, The Pine Lane Hotel or The Pineview Hotel?

182. Can you name Sam's stalker?

183. What 'first' was taking place at the hotel?

184. What are Chuck and Becky drinking at the bar?

185. Becky says that the LARPing has started, what is LARPing?

186. Which two famous musical partnerships are the agents named after?

187. What is the name of the ghost mistress who ran the orphanage years ago?

188. In what way does the barmaid say Dean and Sam are different to the other attendees at the convention?

189. True or false: The ghost mistress allegedly killed three children under her care?

190. Where in the house were the murders committed?

191. What does the ghost child say to Dean and Sam?

192. What do the *Supernatural* fans need to do in the graveyard?

193. What are the two Winchester brother LARPers' real names?

194. How did the above meet?

195. Who does Becky say Lilith gave the Colt to?

Episode 10 – Abandon All Hope…

196. Who do we meet at the beginning of this episode?

197. What does the above have, that Dean and Sam want?

198. Who is Castiel drinking with?

199. What are gathering in the town?

200. Who is in the photograph that Bobby takes at his house?

201. Why does he take the picture?

202. Jo is attacked and fatally injured by what – a demon, a hellhound or a vampire?

203. Who sets the above on the group?

204. What is Lucifer planning to unleash?

205. Who is Lucifer's brother

206. Who dies in Ellen's arms?

207. Who sacrifices themself in the explosion to give the others time to get away?

208. Who does Lucifer kill in order to summon Death to the town?

209. True or false: Lucifer cannot be killed by the Colt?

210. What happens to the photograph that Bobby took?

Kurt Fuller (Zachariah)

211. In which Californian city was Kurt born in 1953 – San Francisco, San Diego or San Jose?

212. In what subject does Kurt have a degree from UC Berkeley?

213. What job did Kurt do before becoming a full-time professional actor?

214. Can you name Kurt's wife, the daughter of an English writer?

215. True or false: Kurt has two sons?

216. How tall is Kurt?

217. Kurt first came to recognition as a stage actor in what play by Steven Berkoff?

218. In what popular American TV series starring Teri Hatcher did Kurt play Detective Barton in 2005-6?

219. Kurt appeared in what 1992 movie with Mike Myers?

220. What was Kurt's character's occupation in the American TV series *Psyche* 2009-14?

221. In what 2003 movie, starring Adam Sandler and Jack Nicholson did Kurt play the role of Frank Head?

222. Which of the following TV series has Kurt *not* appeared in – *Parenthood, The Good Wife* or *Mad Men*?

223. What character did Kurt play in the TV series *Better With You*?

224. How many episodes of *Supernatural* does Kurt's
character, Zachariah, appear in up to the end of
Season 5?

225. In what episode of *Supernatural* Season 5 does
Kurt's character, Zachariah, die?

Episode 11 – Sam, Interrupted

226. Where is this episode set?

227. What does Susan say killed her roommate?

228. Dean describes 'Alex' (Sam), as being high on what substance?

229. In the four month period before Dean and Sam arrive how many people have died – three, four or five?

230. How does the doctor describe Dean and Sam's relationship?

231. What was the former occupation of inmate and friend of John Winchester, Martin Wreath?

232. What do Dean and Sam tell Nurse Foreman they are looking for in the morgue?

233. What kind of brain-eating monster are the brothers up against?

234. Dean sees the reflection of a monster in the mirror, who did it belong to?

235. What does the patient, Wendy, do to Dean?

236. What does the above do to Sam?

237. How do the hunters know that Dr Fuller is not the wraith?

238. How are the victims being poisoned?

239. Who is the real wraith – Wendy, Nurse Foreman or Dr Erica Cartwright?

240. True or false: Sam kills the wraith with a silver bullet?

Episode 12 – Swap Meat

241. At the bar, what kind of daiquiri does Sam order?

242. What is name of the woman at the bar?

243. Who do Dean and Sam visit – their old babysitter, old school teacher or friend of John Winchester's?

244. What is the problem at the house?

245. Who picks Sam up on the road after he has been drugged?

246. True or false: The reflection that Sam sees in the mirror is not his own?

247. What does Gary, posing as Sam, throw away?

248. What does Sam find in Gary's room and locker?

249. What type of plant do Dean and Gary find in the basement of the house that signifies a witch's grave?

250. Who burns the body of Maggie Briggs?

251. Who captures Sam and ties him up?

252. Which rap track by the Wu-Tang Clan does Trevor quote?

253. Nora is possessed by a demon, which duo exorcises her?

254. What 'reward' does the demon offer Trevor?

255. What advice does Sam give Gary?

256. What song by Norman Greenbaum plays when Dean and Sam arrive in the deserted town in episode 2 'Good God, Y'All'?

257. Which Bob Dylan song features in episode 15 'Dead Men Don't Wear plaid' – 'The Times They are a-Changing', 'Knockin' on Heaven's Door' or 'Forever Young'?

258. What game is Dean asking about in episode 7 'The Curious Case of Dean Winchester' when 'I Want All My Money Back' by Lonnie Brooks is playing?

259. What song does Zachariah sing in episode 18 'Point of No Return'?

260. Episode 13 'The Song Remains the Same' features a track called 'The Creeper' by which American hard rock band?

261. What Jen Titus songs features in episode 21 'Two Minutes to Midnight'?

262. The theme tune from which 1980s' TV series featuring a talking car, features in episode 8 'Changing Channels'?

263. What Santana song features in episode 19 'Abandon All Hope'?

264. Which *Supernatural* Season 5 episode features 'Carry on Wayward Son' by Kansas?

265. What song by 'The Contours' features in episode 4 'The End'?

266. Which song by Swank plays in the bar when the
hunters find Sam (posing as Keith) in episode 3
'Free to Be You and Me'?

267. What two songs by The Bughouse Five feature in
episode 9 'The Real Ghostbusters'?

268. How many songs are featured in episode 6 'I believe
the Children Are Our Future'?

269. True or false: Four episodes of *Supernatural* Season
5 have no soundtrack?

270. Which song by Sonny Ellis features in episode 12
'Swap Meat'?

Episode 13 – The Song Remains the Same

271. Where does Anna say that she is being kept a prisoner?

272. Who disbelieves Anna when she says that she has escaped?

273. How does Anna communicate with Dean to let him know where to meet her?

274. What does Anna tell Castiel?

275. What year is Anna in – 1968, 1978 or 1988?

276. What has Anna gone back to do?

277. Why?

278. How does Dean describe the car journey with their parents?

279. Who does Anna summon?

280. Which song by the Beatles did Mary Winchester sing to her sons instead of a lullaby?

281. Who kills Anna – Michael, Castiel or Dean?

282. What does Michael tell Dean is an illusion?

283. What are Castiel, Dean and Sam collectively called (according to Dean)?

284. What does Mary say is watching over her unborn child (Dean)?

285. True or false: According to Michael, Dean and
Sam's bloodline goes back to Cain and Abel?

Episode 14 – My Bloody Valentine

286. How do the first unfortunate couple die?

287. How do the second couple die?

288. What part of the victims' bodies are marked?

289. What kind of 'marks' are they?

290. Who does Castiel think this is a sign of?

291. What is the above wearing when Castiel summons him?

292. True or false: The above is following orders from heaven?

293. How many suicides have there been so far – seven, eight or nine?

294. Which one of the Four Horsemen of the Apocalypse is in town?

295. What is Sam hungry for?

296. Why isn't Dean affected by the Horseman?

297. What is Castiel craving?

298. How does the coroner die?

299. What do Dean and Bobby do to Sam?

300. What does Dean do at the end of the episode?

Kim Rhodes (Jody Mills)

301. True or false: Kim is short for Kimberly

302. In what year was Kim born – 1968, 1969 or 1970?

303. Kim has a Master's degree from Temple University, Philadelphia, in what subject?

304. In how many kinds of stage combat is Kim certified?

305. What pastime is Kim passionate about?

306. What job did Kim have prior to becoming an actress?

307. Which actor did Kim marry in 2006?

308. Can you name Kim's daughter, born in 2008?

309. In what TV series and Disney Channel spin-off did Kim play Carey Martin, from 2008-2011, prior to appearing in *Supernatural*?

310. Kim played Christine in which 2011 short comedy film narrated by John Cleese?

311. What charity is Kim known to support?

312. In what TV movie did Kim play Maureen O'Connor in 2008?

313. Kim played the character of Cindy Harrison in two American soap operas, *Another World* was one, can you name the other?

314. Kim rewrote the lyrics from which *Godspell* song for her first *Another World* fan club function?

315. What is the first episode of *Supernatural* in which we meet Kim's character, Sheriff Jody Mills?

Episode 15 – Dead Men Don't Wear Plaid

316. What is the name of the witness at the beginning of the episode?

317. What does Clay do when he rises from the dead?

318. Can you name the female sheriff?

319. What is the name of Bobby's dead wife – Karen, Kim or Katrina?

320. What does the above do whilst she is cooking?

321. Why does Bobby initially think that his wife and others are returning from the dead?

322. What happens to the people who come back from the dead a few days afterwards?

323. How do Dean and Sam kill the zombies?

324. Why does Bobby send Dean and Sam away?

325. Who kills the sheriff's husband?

326. Where do Dean, Sam and the sheriff take the townspeople to keep them safe?

327. What message does Bobby's wife have for her husband?

328. Who saves Bobby and Dean from the zombies?

329. True or false: Bobby has now killed his wife three times?

330. Why is Death watching Bobby?

Episode 16 – Dark Side of the Moon

331. Which two hunters arrive to shoot Dean and Sam?

332. What do Dean and young Sam do together?

333. Where are Dean and Sam?

334. Who speaks to Dean through the car radio?

335. Who is after Dean and Sam?

336. What does the above tell Dean to follow?

337. What is the name of the angel that Dean and Sam need to find?

338. Why is Dean annoyed by Sam's favourite memories?

339. What was the name of Sam's dog?

340. Who is the masked man that helps Dean and Sam in heaven?

341. Who kisses Dean?

342. Who do Dean and Sam meet at their childhood home?

343. True or false: The above taunts Dean?

344. What special property does Dean's amulet hold?

345. What does Dean do with the amulet?

Julian Richings (Death)

346. In what country was Julian born in 1956?

347. Julian moved to which country in 1984?

348. With a September birthday, what sign of the zodiac was Julian born under?

349. At which UK University did Julian study drama – Durham, Exeter or Oxford?

350. How many children does Julian have?

351. In what American/Canadian TV series did Julian play the role of Ardix in 1989-90?

352. Julian received a Genie Award nomination for Best Supporting Actor for his role as Francis Bellanger in which 2000 British film?

353. What role did Julian play in the Canadian TV Series *Once a Thief* in 1997-98?

354. In what Stephen King TV drama series did Julian play the role of Otto for 13 episodes in 2004?

355. What role did Julian play in the 2010 movie *Percy Jackson and the Lightning Thief*?

356. In what Canadian city does Julian live with his family?

357. True or false: Julian gives classes on acting and movement for actors?

358. Apart from *Supernatural*, Julian also played Death which TV short film?

359. Julian originally read for which role in *Supernatural*?

360. In which episode of *Supernatural* Season 5 does Julian's character Death makes his dramatic entrance?

Episode 17 – 99 Problems

361. What element prevents the Winchester brothers from escaping in the opening scene?

362. What are Dean and Sam trying to escape from?

363. True or false: They are saved by members of the Sacrament Lutheran Militia?

364. There have been eight what held that week – weddings, deaths or exorcisms?

365. What power does Leah Gideon claim to possess?

366. According to Sam, which of the angels' commandments 'wipe out ninety percent' of Dean's personality,?

367. When Castiel arrives what is wrong with him?

368. Where has Castiel been?

369. What happens to Paul, the bartender?

370. The real Leah Gideon is dead, who is posing as her?

371. According to Castiel, with what do you kill the above?

372. Who is the only one who can use this 'weapon'?

373. Who kills her?

374. Why is Sam concerned about Dean?

375. Who does Dean visit at the end of the episode?

Episode 18 – Point of No Return

376. Who is drinking in the bar in the opening scene?

377. Who does Sam take with him as backup when he goes to find Dean?

378. Who is resurrected from the dead?

379. What do the angels tell the above he is going to do?

380. Why was he resurrected?

381. What have the angels promised in return?

382. Where are Sam and Castiel keeping Dean locked up?

383. Who visits Adam in a dream – Castiel, Zachariah or Lucifer?

384. What does Castiel say to the preacher that he knocks out?

385. Where does Zachariah takes Adam?

386. What does Zachariah do to Adam?

387. Where is the green room located?

388. True or false: Zachariah has taken Adam to be Michael's vessel?

389. Who kills Zachariah?

390. Who gets left behind when Dean, Sam and Adam try to escape?

Mark Pellegrino (Lucifer)

391. In what year was Mark born in Los Angeles?

392. What is Mark's middle name – Richard, Reece or Ross ?

393. Can you name Mark's director wife?

394. True or false: Mark enjoys a range of sports including kickboxing, Judo and Karate?

395. What role did Mark play in the 1987 comedy action thriller *Fatal Beauty* starring Whoopi Goldberg?

396. In what American cult movie, written by Joel and Ethan Coen, did Mark play the Blond Treehorn Thug?

397. What American political party is Mark actively involved with?

398. In what long-running American TV drama did Mark play the role of Jacob in 2009-10?

399. What kind of roles is Mark most commonly associated with?

400. Where does Mark teach acting?

401. In what TV drama did Mark play the role of Paul Bennett?

402. Mark went on to play the role of Dr Price in *The Tomorrow People* 2013-14, what was his character's Christian name?

403. Can you name Mark's character in the 2015 TV series *Quantico*?

404. Mark is close friends with which actor who plays
War in *Supernatural* Season 5?

405. What role in *Supernatural* was Mark originally
considered for?

Episode 19 – Hammer of the Gods

406. Can you name the hotel that Dean and Sam book into at the beginning of this episode?

407. What does Dean see in the room as he passes?

408. What kind of soup do Dean and Sam find in the kitchen?

409. Who are the people staying at the hotel?

410. Who is the Archangel Gabriel posing as?

411. True or false: Ghostfacers' new intern is called AJ?

412. What does Kali want that Gabriel has in his possession?

413. What is Gabriel's nickname for Lucifer?

414. Who stabs Gabriel – Baldur, Kali or Ganesh?

415. Why doesn't the sword kill him?

416. Whose side does Gabriel tell Dean and Sam he is on?

417. What DVD does Gabriel ask Dean to 'guard with his life'?

418. What are the keys for Lucifer's trap?

419. How many of the above do Dean and Sam already possess?

420. Which of the Four Horsemen do we see at the end of the episode?

Episode 20 – The Devil You Know

421. What do the doctors believe the disease is that they are dealing with?

422. What name does Crowley call Pestilence – Grumpy, Sneezy or Dopey?

423. Why doesn't Crowley want Sam along?

424. How does Crowley know about Dean and Sam's plans?

425. How does Brady communicate with Pestilence?

426. What do they draw a devil's trap on?

427. How does Sam know the demon, Brady?

428. Who does the possessed Brady introduce Sam to?

429. Why is the above murdered?

430. What is Crowley's nickname for Sam?

431. What does Crowley carve into Brady's chest?

432. How does Crowley describe his relationship with Brady?

433. How does Crowley kill the hellhounds?

434. True or false: Sam kills Pestilence with Ruby's knife?

435. What does Crowley want from Bobby in exchange for information on Death's whereabouts?

Mark Sheppard (Crowley)

436. In what country was Mark born?

437. What is Mark's middle name – Andrew, Andreas or Arthur?

438. What profession did Mark take up, aged 15?

439. True or false: Mark's father is also an actor?

440. How many children does Mark have from his first marriage?

441. Mark was born in May of what year?

442. Can you name the 2012 cinematic adaptation of a Jules Verne novel that Mark directed?

443. What character did Mark play in the TV series *Battlestar Gallactica* (2007-9)?

444. In what TV series did Mark play the role of Curtis Hagen 2009-14?

445. What musical instrument is Mark known for playing?

446. Can you name the character that Mark played in the American TV drama series *Leverage* from 2008-2012?

447. Mark played the role of Paddy Armstrong in the 1993 movie *In the Name of the Father* starring Daniel Day-Lewis and which British actress?

448. With which actor did Mark star in the 1997 movie *Nether World*?

449. In what British TV sci-fi series did Mark play the role of Canton Delaware in 2011?

450. In what episode of *Supernatural* Season 5 does Crowley first appear in person?

Episode 21 – Two Minutes to Midnight

451. What is the name of the doctor at the Serenity Valley Convalescent Home – Dr Black, Dr White or Dr Green?

452. Who is the above in reality?

453. How does Castiel say he got to the convalescent home?

454. Where was he found?

455. What does Dean say Castiel is out of?

456. Who cuts off Pestilence's finger?

457. What does Castiel use to kill Pestilence?

458. What does Bobby give in exchange for Death's location?

459. How do demons close a deal?

460. Who drives into town (Chicago) in a white car?

461. Who describes Lucifer as 'a bratty child having a tantrum'?

462. What does Sam plan to do whilst hosting Lucifer?

463. What virus are people being infected with?

464. What does Death offer to lend Dean in order to trap Lucifer?

465. Why is Death helping Dean?

Episode 22 – Swan Song

466. What does Chuck describe as 'the most important item in the universe'?

467. What is the name of Chuck's manuscript?

468. Why does Sam believe that he should be the one to stop Lucifer?

469. How does Sam 'prepare'?

470. What is strange about the fact that Castiel is sleeping?

471. What does Sam want Dean to promise?

472. What did young Dean push into the vent of the Impala?

473. Where is Lucifer when he possesses Sam?

474. Where is the showdown between Michael and Lucifer due to take place?

475. Who is Michael's vessel?

476. What does Lucifer do to Castiel?

477. Who else is killed by Lucifer?

478. Why does Chuck believe that Dean and Sam passed God's test?

479. Who does Dean turn to at the end of the episode?

480. Who is seen looking in on them at the end of the series?

481. Name the Four Horsemen of the Apocalypse that feature in *Supernatural* Season 5.

482. Which one of the above is known as the Black Horseman?

483. Which one of question 481 above is known as the Red Horseman?

484. Which one of the Four Horsemen wears a green emerald ring?

485. Which one of the Four Horsemen can resurrect the dead?

486. Who wrote the first and last episodes of *Supernatural* Season 5 'Sympathy for the Devil' and 'Swan Song'?

487. True or false: Alistair Crowley is a fictitious name made up for *Supernatural*?

488. The promotion of episode 1 of *Supernatural* Season 5 started a religious argument on Twitter with which American hip hop artist?

489. Can you name the special effects supervisor on *Supernatural*?

490. What writer left *Supernatural* at the end of Season 5 but subsequently returned as an executive producer for Season 8?

491. Can you name the gods and deities that gather at the Elysian Fields Hotel in episode 19 'Hammer of the Gods' to discuss the threat of the Apocalypse?

492. Chuck Shurley's pen name, Carver Edlund is a portmanteau of which two writers on *Supernatural*?

493. Episode 9 'The Real Ghostbusters' was nominated for a GLAAD Media Award for Outstanding Individual Episode in 2010, what American political comedy sitcom did it lose out to?

494. Which episode was the first to be directed by John Showalter?

495. Who took over production during *Supernatural* Season 5?

496. What language is used by angels?

497. Can you name the 100th episode of *Supernatural* Season 5?

498. Who directed the above episode?

499. Can you name the band made up of *Supernatural* cast and crew members that played at the party to celebrate the 100th episode?

500. True or false: *Supernatural* Season 5 was Eric Kripke's last as showrunner?

'I'd say this was a test... for Sam and Dean. And I think they did all right. Up against good, evil, angels, devils, destiny, and God himself, they made their own choice. They chose family. And, well... isn't that kinda the whole point?' ~ Chuck Shurley

Answers

Episode 1 – Sympathy for the Devil

1. Where the last episode of *Supernatural* Season 4 finishes when Lucifer is released from the cage

2. They shut, locking them in the chapel with Lucifer

3. On an aeroplane full of people, with no idea how they got there

4. A beam of white light from the ground to the sky forces the plane into descent

5. He is 'dead or gone' (the Archangels smote him and he exploded)

6. Before he finds his vessel and unleashes hell on Earth (The Four Horsemen)

7. A hex bag (so neither angels nor demons can find them)

8. Becky Rosen (Chuck's number one fan)

9. Michael (an Archangel)

10. An old card of his dad's for a lockup 'Castle Storage 42 Roverhill'

11. Bobby regains control and stabs himself with the demon knife

12. Dean

13. Castiel

14. Lucifer's chosen vessel (Lucifer visits Nick, in the form of his wife, and tells him he will help him get justice for the murder of his family)

15. He is unlikely to walk ever again

Episode 2 – Good God, Y'All

16. Because he is cut off from heaven and can only do certain things

17. That he is going to find God

18. Dean's amulet, that shines bright in God's presence

19. Rufus – he is in a demon-infested town (River Pass, Colorado) and needs help

20. Ellen Harvelle

21. Her daughter, Jo (they have been separated and Ellen is looking for her when she finds Dean and Sam)

22. Because he doesn't want Sam being around demons

23. They don't light up or react in the same way (when he stabs them or to his exorcism)

24. Jo and Rufus

25. A demon (and he thinks they are demons)

26. The Apocalypse (according to the *Bible*). The omens are specific to The Horsemen, particularly War, who makes people believe that others are demons when, in reality, no one is.

27. Through his ring on his finger

28. Red Mustang (aka his horse)

29. By cutting his finger and ring off

30. Take a break from hunting

Episode Titles

31. Abandon All Hope (episode 10) – 'Abandon all hope, ye who enter here'

32. Sam, Interrupted (episode 11) – a reference to *Girl, Interrupted*

33. Two Minutes to Midnight (episode 21)

34. I Believe the Children Are Our Future (episode 6) – lyric from 'The Greatest Love of All'

35. The End (episode 4)

36. Dark Side of the Moon (episode 16)

37. My Bloody Valentine (episode 14)

38. Swan Song (episode 22)

39. Hammer of the Gods (episode 19)

40. The Curious Case of Dean Winchester (episode 7) – from *The Curious Case of Benjamin Button*

41. Sympathy for the Devil (episode 1)

42. 99 Problems (episode 17)

43. The Devil You Know (episode 20)

44. The Song Remains the Same (episode 11)

45. Dead Men Don't Wear Plaid (episode 15)

Episode 3 – Free to Be You and Me

46. Sam's girlfriend, Jessica, who was killed in Season 1
47. All of his fake IDs
48. A bartender
49. Castiel
50. Raphael (to interrogate him)
51. A police badge
52. To a 'den of iniquity' (brothel)
53. Old hunting buddies
54. True
55. His brother
56. That God is dead
57. Lucifer
58. Sam
59. Demon blood
60. A Teenage Mutant Ninja Turtle

Episode 4 – The End

61. Castiel

62. Talking to a messenger of God on a cellphone (like watching a Hells Angel ride a moped)

63. Sam with the news that he is Lucifer's vessel

64. The same hotel room except that it is 2014 and the town is derelict

65. Zachariah

66. Bobby's wheelchair with bullet holes through the back, a photo of Bobby, Castiel and others at a place called Camp Chitaqua

67. Himself in the future – future Dean (2014)

68. Rhonda Hurley made them try on her 'panties', they were pink and satiny and Dean 'kinda liked it'.

69. Chuck

70. He is stoned, surrounded by girls and preparing for an orgy

71. Future Dean says that he is infected with the Croatoan virus

72. To show him that Sam has said 'yes' to Lucifer and is his vessel

73. White

74. Castiel

75. True

76. Death (episode 21 'Two Minutes to Midnight')

77. Bobby (episode 10 'Abandon All Hope')

78. Future Chuck (episode 4 'The End')

79. Crowley (episode 10 'Abandon All Hope…')

80. Adam Milligan (episode 18 'Point of No Return')

81. Dean Winchester (episode 1 'Sympathy for the Devil')

82. Michael (episode 13 'The Song Remains the Same')

83. Demian, Demian and Barnes (episode 9 'The Real Ghostbusters')

84. War, one of the Four Horsemen of the Apocalypse (episode 2 'Good God, Y'All')

85. Sam Winchester (episode 11 'Sam, Interrupted')

86. Karen Singer, Bobby's wife (episode 15 'Dead Men Don't Wear Plaid')

87. Mark Sheppard (on Twitter)

88. Becky Rosen (episode 9 'The Real Ghostbusters')

89. Lucifer (episode 1 'Sympathy for the Devil')

90. Castiel (episode 16 'Dark Side of the Moon')

Episode 5 – Fallen Idols

91. James Dean's

92. Little Bastard 130

93. The radio plays, his breath freezes and this head smashes into the windscreen, killing him

94. Bonham and Copeland, after drummers John Bonham (Led Zeppelin) and Stewart Copeland (Police)

95. To find out the engine number (to see if really is James Dean's Car)

96. False: It is a fake

97. Abraham Lincoln

98. Waxwork museum

99. Possessions from the original owners

100. Ghandi's

101. Paris Hilton

102. Seeds

103. Leshi

104. His father, John Winchester

105. *House of Wax* (2005)

Episode 6 – I Believe the Children Are Our Future

106. The young boy pretending to be dead with a pencil in his head

107. The babysitter dead on the sofa

108. She had (literally) scratched her brains out

109. Put itching powder on his babysitter's hairbrush

110. A man has been fried to death with a joy buzzer (zapper)

111. Uses it to fry a ham which he then eats

112. Her dad had told her about the tooth fairy and she thought it was creepy

113. Put her tooth under his pillow

114. He has his teeth removed by a giant tooth fairy

115. Children with stomach ulcers after mixing Pop Rocks and Coke

116. A young boy named Jesse Turner

117. True

118. That Jesse is half demon

119. Kill him

120. He disappears

Cast Appearances

121. Pestilence

122. Young John Winchester

123. *90210*

124. Emily Perkins

125. Joshua

126. Paris Hilton

127. *Lost*

128. Cupid

129. Hunters (Steve, Reggie and Tim)

130. Whore of Babylon

131. Demian and Barnes

132. *The Good Wife*

133. False: She plays the role of his wife

134. Three friends who play with black magic and encounter demons (Gary Frankel, Nora and Trevor)

135. James Otis

Episode 7 – The Curious Case of Dean Winchester

136. They are becoming old before their time and dying

137. By his tattoo

138. Irish

139. 25 years

140. False: He tells Dean that he must win them back in a poker game

141. Dean

142. Because of his failing eyesight (brought on by old age)

143. The 'clap' (gonorrhoea)

144. Lia, Patrick's girlfriend

145. Yes, 13 years so the he can see his granddaughter's bat mitzvah

146. Sciatica

147. Because Patrick wasn't fooled into using the toothpick to pass on his DNA

148. Sam

149. She misses her deceased daughter

150. She plays Patrick at cards and loses all her years

Episode 8 – Changing Channels

151. A tandem bicycle
152. Cathy
153. The Incredible Hulk
154. Candy wrappers
155. The Trickster
156. *Dr. Sexy M.D.*
157. 24 hours
158. The Nutcracker
159. Castiel
160. True
161. Neither side
162. The Impala
163. With a ring of burning holy oil
164. Gabriel
165. Sam (the rebellious son)

Rob Benedict (Chuck Shurley)

166. Patrick

167. 1970

168. USA (Columbia, Missouri)

169. Amy Benedict

170. Performance Studies

171. James Dean

172. *Head Case*

173. Louden Swain

174. *A Brand New Hurt* (the group's fourth studio album)

175. True

176. *State of Play*

177. Richard Coad

178. Two: Calvin and Audrey

179. Richard Speight Jr

180. Carver Edlund

Episode 9 – The Real Ghostbusters

181. The Pineview Hotel

182. Becky Rosen

183. *Supernatural* convention

184. Yellow-eyed coolers

185. Live Action Role Playing

186. Agents Lennon and McCartney (John Lennon/Paul McCartney from the Beatles) and Agents Jagger and Richards (Mick Jagger/Keith Richards from the Rolling Stones)

187. Mistress (Leticia) Gore

188. They are not scared of girls

189. False: She was reported to have killed four children (but it later transpires that three of the boys killed the ghost mistress's son)

190. The attic

191. My mummy loves me

192. Dig up the boys' bones and burn them

193. Demian and Barnes

194. Through an online *Supernatural* chat room

195. A demon named Crowley

Episode 10 – Abandon All Hope...

196. Crowley

197. The Colt

198. Ellen Harvelle

199. Reapers

200. Bobby, Dean, Sam, Castiel, Ellen and Jo

201. Because it might be their last night on Earth

202. A hellhound

203. Meg

204. The angel of death

205. Michael

206. Her daughter, Jo Harvelle

207. Ellen Harvelle

208. All the women and children

209. True

210. He throws it into the fire (symbolising a hunter's funeral pyre for Ellen and Jo)

Kurt Fuller (Zachariah)

211. San Francisco

212. English Literature

213. Realtor (estate agent)

214. Jessica Hendra (father is Tony Hendra)

215. False: He has two daughters (Julia and Charlotte)

216. 6 ft 3 (1.91 m)

217. *Kvetch*

218. *Desperate Housewives*

219. *Wayne's World*

220. Coroner (Woody Strode)

221. *Anger Management*

222. *Mad Men*

223. Joel Putney

224. Seven

225. Episode 18 'Point of No Return'

Episode 11 – Sam, Interrupted

226. In an asylum (Glenwood Springs Psychiatric Hospital)

227. A monster

228. Demon blood

229. Five

230. Dangerously co-dependent

231. Hunter

232. Pudding

233. A wraith

234. The doctor (Dr Fuller)

235. Kisses him

236. Kisses him also

237. He doesn't react to silver

238. Through saliva

239. Nurse Foreman

240. False: Dean kills the wraith with a silver letter opener

Episode 12 – Swap Meat

241. Banana

242. Crystal

243. Their old babysitter

244. A poltergeist

245. The police

246. True: He sees Gary Frankel's reflection

247. All the mobile phones in Dean's car

248. Items and a book used in witchcraft

249. Willow moss

250. Gary

251. Gary's friends

252. C.R.E.A.M. (Dolla dolla bills y'all)

253. Dean and Gary

254. His undying gratitude

255. Rebel a little bit (in a healthy, non-satanic way)

Supernatural Soundtrack

256. Spirit in the Sky

257. Knockin' on Heaven's Door

258. Poker

259. When the Saints Go Marching In (Kurt Fuller)

260. Molly Hatchet

261. O Death

262. *Knight Rider* (the 'Night Rider theme tune' by Stu Phillips)

263. Oye Como Va

264. Episode 22 'Swan Song'

265. Do You Love Me

266. Devil Sway

267. 'Topsy Turvy' and 'Trouble Baby'

268. None

269. True: Episodes, 6 'I Believe the Children Are Our Future', 11 'Sam, Interrupted', 14 'My Bloody Valentine' and 20 'The Devil You Know'

270. I Got More Bills than I Got Pay

Episode 13 – The Song Remains the Same

271. Heaven

272. Castiel

273. In a dream

274. Sam Winchester has to die

275. 1978

276. Kill Dean and Sam's parents

277. So that Sam won't ever be born

278. An awkward family road trip

279. Uriel

280. Hey Jude

281. Michael

282. Free will

283. Team Free Will

284. Angels

285. True

Episode 14 – My Bloody Valentine

286. They eat each other to death
287. They shoot each other
288. Their hearts
289. Enochian sigils
290. Cupid
291. Nothing, he is naked
292. True
293. Eight
294. Famine
295. Demon blood
296. Because he is empty inside
297. Red meat
298. He drinks himself to death
299. Lock him in Bobby's panic room
300. Pray

Kim Rhodes (Jody Mills)

301. True

302. 1969

303. Fine Arts

304. Four: Hand-to-hand, quarterstaff, rapier and dagger

305. Reading

306. Vet technician's assistant

307. Travis Hodges

308. Tabatha Jane

309. *The Suite Life of Zack and Cody*

310. *Beethoven's Christmas Adventure*

311. American Society for the Prevention of Cruelty to Animals

312. *A Kiss at Midnight*

313. *As the World Turns*

314. All the Best

315. Season 5, episode 15 'Dead Men Don't Wear Plaid'

Episode 15 – Dead Men Don't Wear Plaid

316. Digger

317. Gets revenge on his killer

318. Sheriff Jody Mills

319. Karen

320. Hums

321. It is a sign of the Apocalypse (as told in Revelation)

322. They develop a fever, get hungry and start eating people

323. Shoot them in the head

324. They have come to kill his wife

325. Her son, who has risen from the dead

326. The local jail

327. Death has come for him (Bobby)

328. Sam and sheriff Mills

329. False: He has killed her twice

330. Because he is helping Sam to resist Lucifer

Episode 16 – Dark Side of the Moon

331. Walt and Roy

332. Let off fireworks

333. In heaven

334. Castiel

335. Zachariah

336. The road

337. Joshua

338. They all involve leaving him (Dean)

339. Bones

340. Ash

341. Pamela Barnes

342. Their mother, Mary Winchester

343. True: Saying it is his own fault that everyone leaves him

344. It glows in God's presence

345. Throws it in the bin

Julian Richings (Death)

346. England (Oxford)

347. Canada

348. Virgo

349. Exeter

350. Two (a son and a daughter)

351. *War of the Worlds*

352. *The Claim*

353. Camier

354. *Kingdom Hospital*

355. The Ferryman

356. Toronto

357. True

358. *Dave vs Death*

359. Pestilence

360. Episode 21 'Two Minutes to Midnight'

Episode 17 – 99 Problems

361. Fire

362. Demons

363. True

364. Weddings

365. She receives prophetic visions from the angels

366. No drinking, no pre-marital sex, no gambling

367. He is drunk

368. On a bender

369. He is shot and killed (by Jane)

370. The Whore of Babylon

371. A cypress branch

372. A 'true servant of heaven'

373. Dean

374. He thinks that Dean might be considering accepting Michael's proposal to be his vessel

375. Lisa Braeden

Episode 18 – Point of No Return

376. Zachariah

377. Castiel

378. Adam Milligan, Dean and Sam's half-brother

379. Save the world

380. To be Michael's vessel

381. To bring his mother back from the dead

382. In Bobby's panic room

383. Zachariah

384. "You pray too loud"

385. To the 'green room'

386. Makes him cough up blood

387. Van Nuys, California

388. False: It is a trap for Dean

389. Dean

390. Adam

Mark Pellegrino (Lucifer)

391. 1965

392. Ross

393. Tracy Aziz (born Tracy Bell)

394. True

395. Frankenstein

396. *The Big Lebowski*

397. The American Capitalist Party

398. *Lost*

399. Villainous roles

400. Playhouse West (founded by Robert Carnegie)

401. *Dexter*

402. Jedikiah

403. Clayton Haas

404. Titus Welliver

405. Castiel

Episode 19 – Hammer of the Gods

406. The Elysian Fields Hotel

407. An elephant

408. Eyeball

409. Gods

410. Loki (the Trickster)

411. True

412. Angel blade

413. Lucy

414. Kali

415. It is a fake

416. Humans

417. *Casa Erotica*

418. The rings of the Four Horsemen of the Apocalypse

419. Two: Those belonging to War and Famine

420. Pestilence

Episode 20 – The Devil You Know

421. Swine flu

422. Sneezy

423. Sam keeps trying to kill him

424. He has hidden a magical coin in the Impala to track
their movements and eavesdrop on their
conversations

425. Through a goblet of blood

426. A paper bag

427. They went to college together at Stanford

428. Jessica Moore, his college girlfriend

429. To force Sam back into hunting

430. Moose

431. A binding link (to prevent him from leaving his
'meatsuit')

432. Lovers in league against Satan

433. With a bigger hellhound

434. True

435. His soul

Mark Sheppard (Crowley)

436. England (London)

437. Andreas

438. Musician

439. True: W. Morgan Sheppard

440. Two sons: Max and William

441. 1964

442. *Mysterious Island* (from the 1874 novel *The Mysterious Island*)

443. Romo Lampkin

444. *White Collar*

445. Drums

446. Jim Sterling

447. Emma Thompson

448. His father, W. Morgan Sheppard

449. *Dr Who*

450. Episode 10 'Abandon All Hope'

Episode 21 – Two Minutes to Midnight

451. Dr Green

452. Pestilence

453. By bus

454. On a fishing boat (in Illinois)

455. Angel mojo

456. Castiel

457. Ruby's knife

458. His soul

459. With a kiss

460. Death (the White Horseman)

461. Death

462. Jump into Lucifer's cage (to trap him again)

463. Croatoan

464. His ring

465. Because since Lucifer rose Death has been bound to him and he wants to be free

Episode 22 – Swan Song

466. The Impala

467. Swan Song

468. Because he was the one who released him from hell

469. By drinking lots of demon blood

470. Angels don't sleep

471. Not to bring him back

472. Lego

473. Detroit

474. Stull Cemetery, near Lawrence, Kansas

475. Adam, Dean and Sam's half-brother

476. Blow him up

477. Bobby

478. They chose family over all else

479. Lisa Braeden

480. Sam

481. War, Famine, Pestilence and Death

482. Famine

483. War

484. Pestilence

485. Death

486. Eric Kripke

487. False: Aleister Crowley is the name of real life, notorious English occultist

488. P. Diddy

489. Randy Shymkwi

490. Jeremy Carver

491. Kali, Baldur, Baron Samedi, Ganesh, Odin. Mercury, Zao Shen and Loki (the Trickster)

492. Jeremy Carver and Ben Edlund

493. *Parks and Recreation* (episode 'Pawnee Zoo')

494. Episode 15 'Dead Men Don't Wear Plaid'

495. Jim Michaels

496. Enochian

497. Episode 18 'Point of No return'

498. Phil Sgriccia

499. The Impalas

500. True

Also by
Light Bulb Quizzes

The Supernatural Quiz Book
Seasons 1, 2, 3 and 4

Coming soon
The Supernatural Quiz Book Season 6

Follow Light Bulb Quizzes on

Twitter: @LightBulbQuiz

and

Facebook.com/Lightbulbquizzes

For news, giveaways

and forthcoming projects